JR. CHAPTER BOOK

THE
BAILEY SCHOOL
KIDS®

JR. CHAPTER BOOK

THE BAILEY SCHOOL KIDS®

SNOW MONSTERS DO DRINK HOT CHOCOLATE

by Marcia Thornton Jones and Debbie Dadey
Illustrated by Joëlle Dreidemy

SCHOLASTIC INC.

New York Toronto London Auckland Sydney
Mexico City New Delhi Hong Kong Buenos Aires

To Beverly Young and Eddie Phipps,
two people who are great at what they do and
who truly make a difference every single day.—M.T.J.

To Eric Dadey—God bless you for putting up with me
for 25 wonderful and chaotic years.—D.D.

To Matthieu, alias "Japhy Rider,"
the Ischgl Snow Monster.—J.D.

ISBN-13: 978-0-545-06990-8
ISBN-10: 0-545-06990-4

12   12 13 14/0

Printed in the U.S.A.
First printing, January 2009

CONTENTS

1

FLIPPED OUT

"That is so cool!"
Howie said.

"Wow!" Melody put
down her sled to watch.

"Look at that!" added
Liza.

The four kids were heading up Dedman Hill. All around them kids were sledding. A few kids, like Eddie, used snowboards. But Melody, Howie, Liza, and Eddie weren't looking at a kid. They were watching a grown-up on a snowboard.

Zoom! The grown-up sped down the hill.

Swish! His snowboard left the ground.

Whoosh! He flipped through the air.

"That guy should be on TV," Melody said.

Eddie hugged his snowboard. "I want to do that!"

Liza shook her head. "You could get hurt. Those tricks are too dangerous!"

"I won't get hurt. I'm going to get him to teach ME how to do a flip!" Eddie said. But before he could race over, Howie grabbed Eddie's scarf.

Howie shook his head. "Be careful. That guy has probably practiced for years and years."

"Now look what you've done," Eddie snapped. "All your talking made me miss my chance. He's leaving." The kids watched as the snowboarder took off his hat and goggles. His long white hair was covered with snowflakes. Snow fell over his face and shoulders.

"It's about time he went home," Melody said. "It looks like he's been here all day."

Howie nodded. "There's so much snow on him he looks like a snowman," he said.

"I'm sorry you didn't get to talk to him," Liza said and patted Eddie on the back.

Eddie pulled away from his friends. "Maybe it's not too late. I can still catch him," he cried.

"Wait!" Melody called.

But Eddie NEVER liked to wait.

WAIT!

2
SNOW MONSTER

Eddie took off as fast as he could, but he forgot one thing. The snow.

His boot slipped.

"AHHH!" he screamed. He teetered. He tottered. His feet went one way.

SWOOSH!

The rest of him went the other way.

WHAM!

Eddie landed on his back and slid down the hill.

"Help!" Eddie screamed.
Down, down, down Eddie
rolled. By the time he reached
the bottom of the hill, snow
covered the top of his head.
Snow stuck to his mittens, coat,
and boots.

Eddie's friends sledded
down the hill to join him. "Eddie,
you look like a snowman," Liza
told him.

"More like an abominable
snowman," Melody said with
a giggle.

"Or a snow monster,"
Howie added.

"V-v-very f-f-funny." Eddie
shivered.

"You're freezing," Liza said
as she helped him up. "We
need to warm you up. Fast!"

"I know just the thing,"
Eddie said. "Hot chocolate!"

"Great idea," said Liza.
"Let's see if your grandmother
will take us to Burger Doodle."

"I need chocolate," Eddie said to his grandmother as he opened the door to her van. "Hot chocolate. And FAST!"

He plopped onto the backseat. Melody, Liza, and Howie tumbled in after their friend.

Snow dripped off Eddie's nose, hair, and mittens.

"Eddie doesn't look like a snow monster now," Liza said. Melody shook her head. "He looks like a drowned rat!"

His friends giggled as Eddie's grandmother headed down the street to Burger Doodle.

As soon as they pulled into a parking space, Eddie was out of his seat. He crawled over Howie and out the door of the van. His three friends hurried to catch up.

"Hot chocolate," Eddie chanted. "Must have hot chocolate!"

Eddie ran straight to the door without watching where he was going. Bam! He slammed into something big and white.

3

HARRY SNOWDEN

Eddie looked up into the face of the snowboarder from the hill. He had a face as pale as a snowflake. His jacket and snow pants were as white as the clouds in the sky. Icicles still hung from his hair. There was even a puddle of melting ice by his furry white boots.

The snowboarder reached out to keep Eddie from slipping. Eddie noticed the man's body felt like a solid block of ice.

"Careful," the man said. "Ice can be slippery."

"I hate ice," Eddie snapped.

The man took a step back.

"Hate ice?" he said. "How can anyone hate ice? Hating ice is like saying you hate Christmas and Valentine's Day, or candy and cookies!"

Eddie opened his mouth to argue, but before he could say anything Eddie's grandmother and his friends caught up to him.

"How do you do?" Eddie's grandmother said. "I hope my grandson wasn't bothering you."

"Of course not," the man said.

"My name is Harry Snowden," he said, reaching out to shake Eddie's grandmother's hand.

"Oh, my," Eddie's grandmother said. "You're as cold as your name."

"I love the cold!" Harry told them. "This is the kind of weather I LIVE for."

Howie took a step back. Harry Snowden's breath left clouds in the air between them.

"Well, it was nice meeting you," Eddie's grandmother said. "Come on, kids, let's go inside and have some hot chocolate."

"Now you're talking," Eddie said.

"I've never had hot chocolate, but I do love cold shakes," Harry said. "Is hot chocolate good?"

"It's great!" Eddie yelled.

Howie took a close look at Harry as heavy snow started falling over Burger Doodle. "Hmmm," he said to himself.

But his friends had already followed Eddie inside. Howie's thoughts floated away and were lost in the falling snow.

4

SPLASH!

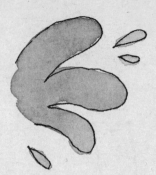

"Here are our drinks,"
Eddie's grandmother said. The
five of them sipped their hot
chocolate without talking.

Howie held his warm cup,
but he kept looking over the
steam at Harry.
Harry sat by himself.
In fact, all the seats
around Harry were
empty. When a
waiter walked by,
Howie saw that
he shivered.

Howie tapped his chin. He scratched his head. He thought and thought and thought some more. Something about Harry Snowden bothered Howie. Something bothered him a lot.

Eddie wasn't looking at Harry. Eddie was looking at the marshmallows floating on the top of Howie's hot chocolate.

"If you're not going to drink that, can I have those marshmallows?" Eddie asked. Without waiting for an answer, Eddie reached for Howie's mug.

Splash! Howie's cup tipped over. Hot chocolate spilled onto the table. Liza grabbed the mug just in time to save some of Howie's drink.

"Oops," Eddie said. "Sorry."

Eddie's grandmother frowned. "I'm going to get napkins to clean up this mess. You behave while I'm gone," she said while looking directly at Eddie.

Eddie groaned. He didn't like to behave, just like he didn't like to wait.

Howie didn't care about his hot chocolate. He was still busy watching Harry Snowden. He took a sip from his mug and then gasped.

"What's wrong?" Liza asked.

"Did the hot chocolate burn your tongue?" Melody asked.

"No, but I have something crazy to tell you," Howie said.

"Do you play with dolls?" Eddie asked.

"No!" Howie said.

"Do you eat bugs?" Liza asked.

"No!" Howie said.

"Do you sleep with a teddy bear?" Melody asked.

"No!" Howie snapped. "But even if I did, I wouldn't tell you!"

"Then what is it?" Melody asked.

"It's Harry," Howie said. "I think he's a snowman."

The four kids glanced at Harry sipping his milk shake. Eddie laughed. "Where's his corncob pipe and carrot nose?"

Howie shook his head. "Not that kind of snowman. I'm talking about an abominable snowman. A yeti. They're

secret monsters that hide in the mountains or woods. But now one has come to Bailey City."

The kids looked at Harry again. He chugged another cold milk shake. Ice still hung from his hair, and now a big puddle of water formed around his boots.

"You are silly," Eddie said. "He's not a monster, and I can prove it."

"How?" Howie asked.

"Easy," Eddie said. "Watch and learn!"

5

CLUMSY

Eddie darted around a table. He hopped over a chair. He nearly bumped a waiter with a tray of hot chocolate mugs.

The closer Eddie got to Harry, the chillier the air was. Eddie's breath came out in quick clouds of cold air as he sneaked up behind Harry.

"Eddie, no!" Liza squeaked.

Just then, Eddie's foot splashed in the puddle around Harry's chair. Only it wasn't a puddle anymore. It had turned to ice. "Yikes!" Eddie yelled as his foot slipped.

Without even turning around, Harry grabbed for  Eddie and stood up. He lifted Eddie off the floor.

"Oh, my. Oh, my, my, my!" Eddie's grandmother said as she rushed over.

Harry slowly lowered Eddie to the floor. "No worries," Harry said. "I just helped your grandson before he slipped on the ice. Again."

The tips of Eddie's ears turned bright red. Eddie's grandmother looked at Eddie.

"Well?" she said. "Don't you have something to say to this kind man?"

Eddie was clueless. "Um, your hands are cold," he told Harry.

Eddie's grandmother poked him in the arm. "Mr. Snowden just helped you," she reminded him. "What do you say?"

Eddie thought and thought and thought some more. Finally, Liza came up and whispered in his ear.

"Oh! I get it," Eddie said. "Thanks!"

"And now I think it's time for me to get you kids home," said Eddie's grandmother, "before we get snowed in. Say good-bye to Mr. Snowden."

" 'Bye," the kids said as they headed out the door.

Snow covered the roads. Snow was piled on cars. Flakes swirled through the air.

"It's going to snow forever!" Melody said with a giggle.

"That," Howie said, "is exactly what I'm afraid of!"

6
FOREVER WINTER

It snowed all afternoon.

It snowed all the next day.

It snowed and snowed and snowed.

"Yippeeeee! No school!" Eddie yelled when he met his friends at Dedman Hill. Liza and Melody were making snow angels. Howie stood off to the side and stared at the sledders racing down the hill.

YIPPEEE!

Blam!
Eddie tossed
a snowball at
Melody.

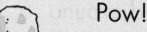

Pow!
Eddie tossed a
snowball at Liza.

Melody and Liza threw
snowballs back. Plop! Liza's
snowball fell in the snow by
Eddie's feet.

Smack! Melody's snowball
landed right on Eddie's
shoulder.

Howie didn't even notice. His face was as pale as the snow on the ground.

"What's wrong?" Liza asked as the three kids huddled around Howie.

"The snow," Howie said.

Eddie nodded. "Isn't it great?"

Eddie grinned. He clapped his hands. He did a happy dance.

"School will be closed forever!" he yelled.

Howie grabbed Eddie's arm to stop his happy dance. "Don't you get it?" Howie asked. "This is the work of a monster. A snow monster named Harry."

"Do you really think he has something to do with it?" Melody asked.

Howie looked at his friends. "I do. Not only is Harry a snow monster, but he's brought winter to Bailey City. And as long as he's here, there will be no sunshine. No spring. No flowers. We'll be stuck with winter forever."

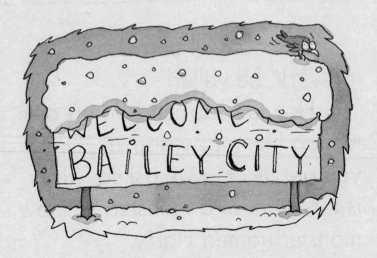

Liza gasped. "That's terrible! We have to do something!"

Melody put her hands on her hips. "I'm not saying I believe Howie," she said, "but I know how we can prove it one way or the other."

"How?" Liza asked.

"Easy," she said. "A snow monster wouldn't like hot things, right? We just have to get him near something hot."

Eddie slapped Melody on the back. "Good idea. Let's do it." Then Eddie stomped away through the snow.

"Wait!" Melody said. "We need to make a plan."

7

WAIT!

"Where are you going?" Liza asked Eddie.

"I'm looking for something warm," Eddie said, staring at the snowy hillside. "But all I see is snow."

"That's why we need to think," Melody told Eddie.

Eddie stuck out his tongue and a snowflake landed on it. "Thinking is boring."

47

"I know something that's warm that might work," Howie told his friends. But just then a snowboarder whizzed past them.

"Look!" Liza pointed. "There's Harry again."

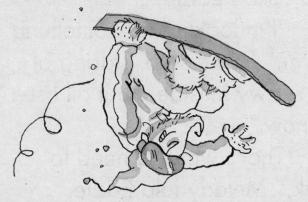

The kids stared as Harry flew into the air on his snowboard and flipped upside down. Every sledder on the hillside gasped.

"Wow!" Eddie screamed.
"That is so cool. I don't care if
he is a snow monster. I want him
to teach me how to do that!"

"Wait!" Howie yelled.

But Eddie ran as fast as he
could toward Harry.

8

GOOSE BUMPS

Wham! Melody tackled Eddie.

Bam! Howie grabbed Eddie's legs.

Smack! Liza jumped on Eddie's head.

"Get off me!" Eddie yelled.

"Not until you promise to stay away from Harry," Liza said. "You could get hurt."

Eddie groaned. "You guys are no fun."

"We're your friends," Melody told him. "It's our job to keep you safe."

"It's also our job to keep you from freezing," Liza said. "I'm so cold my goose bumps have goose bumps."

Melody looked at Harry as he landed on top of a big pile of snow. She shivered. "Only a snow monster could stay out in this cold all day long."

Liza sniffed. "I don't want to go to sleep tonight with a snow monster on the loose. I'm scared."

"Don't worry. What's he going to do? Snow on you?" Eddie teased.

Liza put her hands on her hips. "You won't think it's funny when the snow covers your head. Your house. The candy store!"

Eddie grabbed his chest and fell into the snow. "No! Not the candy store!"

"I think I have an idea," said Howie.

"Is it a way to stop the snow?" asked Liza.

"No, but it's a way we can see if Harry really is a snow monster," replied Howie. "Come on, let's go to my house."

HOT CHOCOLATE MAN

"I am Hot Chocolate Man!" Eddie yelled. He stood on a chair in Howie's kitchen. Howie's mom had made hot chocolate for everyone. Howie was busy pouring some into a thermos.

"You are a crazy kid," Liza told him.

Eddie held his arms over his head. "No, hot chocolate gives me super powers. I can jump over tall hills."

Eddie made a fist. "I can outrun a train."

Eddie hit his fist into his other hand. "I can beat up bad guys."

Melody shook her head. "Can you make it stop snowing?"

Melody looked out the window. It was white everywhere.

"We have to figure out what to do," she said.

Howie nodded. He held up the thermos of hot chocolate. "This is my idea." Eddie didn't wait to hear the rest of the plan. He was already pulling his snow boots back on.

10

GULP!

Liza, Melody, and Howie followed Eddie all the way to the hill. Most sledders had gone home because it was so cold. Not Harry. He was still doing tricks with his snowboard.

Eddie stared at Harry. "He's amazing," Eddie said. "He should be in the Olympics."

"Do they allow snow
monsters in the Olympics?"
Melody asked.

"They'll probably have
to cancel the Olympics and
everything else," Liza said. "If
it keeps snowing, there won't
even be spring soccer!"

Melody and Eddie both
gasped. They loved playing
soccer. "Can nothing stop this
snow monster?" Eddie asked.

"I know what can," Howie
said. He held up the thermos of
hot chocolate.

"Give me that!" Eddie said.

Eddie reached to pull the thermos away from Howie.

"It's not for you, it's for Harry. If he really is a snow monster, he won't be able to drink anything hot." Howie began to pour some hot chocolate into a cup.

"But I want some!" Eddie said and grabbed for the cup. Howie held the cup back, but Eddie pulled harder. The cup flew through the air.

Just then, Harry soared by. He reached out his hand and grabbed the cup.

Harry skidded to a stop.
He sipped the hot chocolate
that was left in the cup. "Wow!
That's good!" he said. "Do you
have any more?"

Howie poured more hot
chocolate into Harry's cup.

Gulp. The snow on Harry's
cap melted.

Gulp. Gulp. The icicles
hanging from Harry's beard
dripped.

GULP! GULP! GULP! The
snow under Harry's boots turned
to slush.

GULP GULP GULP

"That was GREAT!" Harry
roared. "I have to get some
more hot chocolate!"

Harry jumped on his
snowboard and raced down
the hill.

"Oh, no!" Eddie said. "I
still need to get him to teach me
snowboarding tricks. If I hurry, I
can catch him before he melts!"

Liza giggled. "I guess he isn't a snow monster after all."

Howie shrugged. "Either that or snow monsters do drink hot chocolate."

"At least they do now!" Melody said.